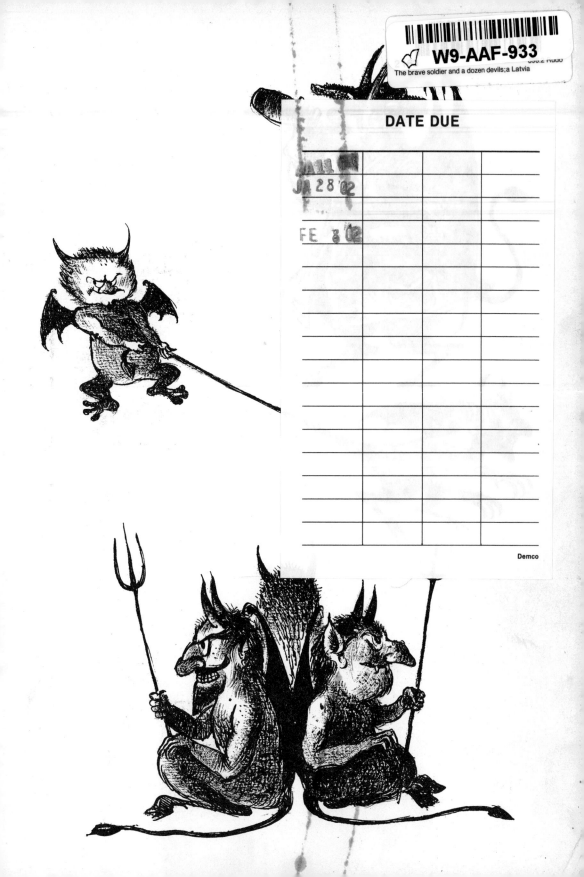

DATE DUE

JA 28 '02		
FE 8 02		

Demco

ALSO BY MARGUERITA RUDOLPH
WITH PICTURES BY IMERO GOBBATO

I am your misfortune

the BRAVE SOLDIER and a DOZEN DEVILS

A LATVIAN TALE

RETOLD BY MARGUERITA RUDOLPH

ILLUSTRATED BY IMERO GOBBATO

THE SEABURY PRESS

New York

Text copyright © 1970 by Marguerita Rudolph
Illustrations copyright © 1970 by Imero Gobbato
Library of Congress Catalog Card Number: 79-115781
All rights reserved. Printed in the U.S.A.

ONCE THERE WAS a young soldier who had finished his years of service in the army. He could now go to any corner of the land—north, south, east, or west. Only he didn't know which direction to take.

The soldier wasn't a fellow to hesitate for long, so he walked straight south on a wide rough road. Soon he came to a spot where it divided. The soldier scratched his head. One way might lead him to friends, and the other might bring him danger. Left? Right? The soldier took a left turn and walked briskly on.

Soon he noticed that there were no boot prints on the road, no ruts from wagon wheels, no horse tracks. And there wasn't a village or a hamlet in sight. Although the soldier was cheerful by nature, this gave him a lonely feeling.

After a while, the soldier became hungry—quite

hungry! But where could he get any food in a place like this? "If only somebody would come along," he said to himself. "Whoever he is, he would surely take kindly to a man in uniform."

Then, as he looked up, the figure of a tall old man appeared over a hill just ahead. The man had

long gray hair and was wearing a purple sash around his tattered coat.

When they came close to each other, the old man spoke:

"What's the matter, soldier? Why do you walk so sadly?"

"How can I be happy," answered the soldier, "when my stomach is empty! I do have three coins and would like to buy a piece of bread. But who's there to sell it to me in such a forsaken place?"

"Why, you have nothing to complain about," said the old man. "Three coins are three more than I have. Perhaps you'll share one of them with me?"

The soldier hesitated a moment. How would he buy bread without money? But he felt sorry for the old man, so he turned to him and said kindly: "I can see you are worse off than I. Here, take one."

The old man put the coin in his pocket. Then he said: "Look here—I seem to have something tucked away. Maybe you'll find use for it." And he pulled out a pipe.

"Oho!" exclaimed the soldier. "A pipe is a soldier's first friend! I am much obliged to you, old man, and wish you the best of health!"

The soldier lighted the pipe and walked on down

the dusty road. He smoked and smoked—and the strangest thing happened. All the tobacco remained in the pipe. It couldn't be smoked out.

"What's going on here?" the soldier thought. "This is surely no ordinary little pipe! All I need now is a sort of bread that could be eaten and eaten and never eaten up!"

As soon as he thought this, he noticed another man approaching him. This one was old and gray like the first. But he was shorter and more weary, and was leaning on a strong stick.

"Good day, soldier," said the old man in a low voice. "You look troubled. What's on your mind?"

"Food!" the soldier answered. "That's the truth, old man. I have a pipe, but it doesn't fill my stomach. And I can scrape up two coins. But I don't have even a crust of bread."

"Well! You are not so badly off, my son. Two coins are two more than I have. Perhaps you'd give me one of them?"

"I'd like to help you," the soldier answered. "But what will I do for money myself?"

"You'd still have one coin left," the old man reasoned.

"That's true," the soldier agreed. "Here, take this one."

The old man slipped the coin into his pocket, then said suddenly: "Wait a minute, soldier. I have something here that you might like." And the old man pulled out of his pocket a small bottle of wine.

"What a present!" the soldier exclaimed. "I do like it, old man. Thank you!"

The soldier put the bottle of wine in his pocket and walked farther along the road. After a while, feeling hungrier than ever, he decided to have a sip from the bottle. He took one sip and another, then looked at the bottle in the light. How odd. None of the wine was gone!

"Oho!" he thought. "This is no ordinary bottle, either. I couldn't drink it to the bottom in a lifetime. Now if only I had a good snack to go with the wine, life would be perfect!"

As soon as he thought this, he noticed a third old man coming toward him. The man carried an empty sack on his back and walked so slowly he seemed to be barely moving. As he came closer, the old man looked into the soldier's face with his large, piercing eyes and asked:

"Why aren't you happy, soldier? Something

must be worrying you."

"Nothing's worrying me," the soldier answered. "But I haven't eaten anything since early morning."

"Too bad." The old man nodded his head. "Don't you have anything in your pocket?"

"Yes," the soldier answered. "I have a pipe and a bottle of wine, and I have one coin besides. But not a crust of bread."

"Oh, you are not so badly off. Indeed not—I don't have anything at all. Maybe you'll help out an old man, and give me your coin."

"But it's my last one!" replied the soldier. "If I give it away I won't be able to buy any bread."

The mention of bread made the soldier hungrier than ever. But the old man's eyes were so sad and his outstretched hand so wrinkled. The soldier took pity on him and handed him his last coin.

The old man nodded gratefully, hid the coin in his coat, and said:

"Thank you, soldier. Now I should give *you* a present. But I don't know what . . . Perhaps this will do."

The old man took the linen sack off his shoulder and gave it to the soldier. "You might have a use for it," he said, and walked away.

The soldier walked on, too, thinking: "Now of what use could an empty sack be?" As soon as he thought this he noticed a fine horse harnessed to a wagon moving toward him on the road. The wagon was loaded with everything imaginable. Mountains of white rolls, big rings of sausages, baskets with roast geese, chunks of pork fat, and rounds of cheese. The driver was not on the wagon. He stood beside the horse, prodding him with a whip.

"He must be taking his master's goods to market," the soldier decided. At the sight of all that food, he felt a dreadful gnawing at the pit of his stomach. He shook his sack and sighed. "Ekh! The rich man's wagon is full to overflowing while I, a poor soldier, have only an empty sack. How I wish I could have just one small loaf of bread and a little piece of pork fat!"

As soon as he said that, a round loaf rolled out of the back of the wagon. And after the loaf came a

chunky piece of pork fat. *Flip-flop*, they tumbled
into the soldier's sack, and the driver didn't see.

The soldier took a small bite of the good bread. Then he quickly put the rest back into the sack to eat later.

He hadn't walked far when he came to the rich man's lands. High fences stretched along the road, protecting the orchards and barns, and ahead was a wide gate with iron bars. The soldier was surprised to see that the gate was open. And the master himself was standing beside it.

"Where are you going, soldier, with night coming on?" he called. "Why don't you sleep over in my house? Rest up from your travels."

This was unheard of! A rich man talking with a plain soldier as if he were his brother?

"I wonder what he is after?" the soldier thought. But he pulled himself up to his full height and made a proper salute.

"Thank you, sir, thank you. With your kind permission, I'll be grateful to sleep in a corner somewhere."

The rich man closed the gate behind them and pulled the heavy latch across it. Then he led the way to his big house. A dog chained in the yard came over to lick the master's hand.

"He must be a very rich man," the soldier thought. He was curious to know how he had come by all his wealth, but this wasn't the time to ask questions.

As soon as they entered the house the master summoned a servant by ringing a bell. The servant must have been very near, for he popped right into the hall. He bowed, waiting for orders.

The master winked at him and said: "Take the soldier up the stairs to the round tower—you know where. Let him enjoy a soft bed."

As he followed the servant, the soldier's stomach began to growl again. He was eager to be left alone so that he could eat his supper at last. When they got to the tower, the servant let the soldier enter, then closed the door behind him. Before the soldier could even turn around—*click!*—the servant snapped the lock on the door.

The soldier was startled. "What's the meaning of locking me up?" he thought. "Is this a jail?" But as he looked around the room, the soldier saw that it couldn't be. It was too large and clean, with rich rugs on the floor and tapestries on the walls.

"This must be the master's own bedroom," the soldier decided. "Look at that bed!"

It stood on a platform in the corner and thick curtains were draped from the top. The soldier had never seen such a bed before. He pressed the mattress with his hands and it was so soft that they sank in.

"It must be filled with down," he thought. "Why isn't the master sleeping in it himself? But that's his business. My business is to eat supper first, then have a good sleep. Stay in bed as long as I like for a change!"

He untied the sack, put his provisions on the table,

and at last started eating. Suddenly he heard a strange noise, then many voices whispering behind the door. The soldier was so surprised that he almost choked on a piece of pork. "What kind of guests can be coming to see me at midnight?" he wondered.

At that moment the locked door swung open and twelve devils tumbled into the room. An even dozen devils, all wagging their tails! Those in the back were leaning on the ones in front. And all of them were stomping with their hoofs, showing their claws, and yelping:

> *Ibbery, jibbery—DOOM*
> *Umpetty, jumpetty—BOOM*
> *Stuffy*
> *Tuffy*
> *PHEW!*

The soldier stared in amazement at the devils.

Then the biggest of them, the chief, looked the soldier over and said: "Who are you? This is the master's bedroom and *he* should be here himself!"

"If it's the master you want, I can help you find him," the soldier offered eagerly. "He is somewhere in this house."

"No!" the devil chief shouted. "According to the agreement, he is supposed to come to *this room.*"

"The rich man has tricked us again," another devil snickered, and he clapped his hands.

"Last year at this time an old beggar was here," a third devil reminded them. And he held up one hairy finger.

"And the year before—a miserable wanderer," still another devil remembered.

"And now—this worthless soldier!" squeaked a small devil, and he stuck his tongue out.

"If I am worthless," the soldier suggested, "why don't you leave me alone?"

The big devil laughed. "Worthless or not, you will be better than nothing."

The devils gathered around the soldier. They hopped from spot to spot, bared their teeth, and

waited for orders from the leader.

"What will they do to me?" the soldier asked himself. He felt terrified. But then he thought: "So the rich man trapped me. He must have made a deal with the devils, and he wants me to suffer for him. Well, I won't!"

The soldier became angry. "I've seen danger and faced death before," he told himself. "So why should I be afraid of some measly devils? They can't take *me!*"

Now he felt no more fear. He straightened himself up as a soldier should and said politely to the devils: "You are my guests. Sit down at the table and have a bite of supper."

"Oh, no, soldier," the leader answered. "It won't do for us to eat leftovers from somebody else's table. We'll have our meal later."

But the soldier didn't lose his wits. He pulled the pipe out of his pocket and said, "Suit yourself. But perhaps you'd like to smoke a little before going home to eat. My grandfather never came to the table without first having a good smoke. And you should have seen the appetite he worked up! You could serve him a whole calf. Come on, have a smoke. My pipe is ready."

Now the devils happened to be very fond of tobacco.

"All right," said the devil chief. "You'll never be able to get away from us anyway—in case you are thinking about it."

So—*pft!* The soldier lighted the pipe and passed it to the chief.

"That's good tobacco, but it's strong," the soldier warned. "Since you are not used to it you may not be able to finish the pipe."

"What do you mean—we won't be able to fin-ish?" The devil chief was offended. "Take it up, fellows," he ordered the other devils, "and don't let go of the pipe till all the tobacco is gone!"

The devils seated themselves in a ring and began

smoking. One devil would take a puff on the pipe and pass it to the next one, and so it went. Smoke filled the room until you could hardly breathe. The soldier had to cover his head with his army coat. The devils kept on smoking, but there was still tobacco in the pipe.

An hour went by, another, and a third. Then suddenly a cock crowed outside the window.

The devil chief jumped up, threw down the pipe, and shouted in alarm: "Oh! It is getting light already!"

Devils have a very strict rule. They can only go about their business from exactly midnight until just before daylight. Never *in* daylight. So all the devils jumped up and ran out of the room pell-mell, coughing and spitting. At the door the devil chief called to the soldier: "We are not finished with you. You'll see us again!"

"What will happen another time doesn't worry me," the soldier answered, but the devils didn't hear him. They had disappeared. The soldier was so glad to see them go, and so tired, that he climbed up on the bed and at once fell into a deep sleep.

At midday the servant came with a broom and a feather duster. He expected to find the room empty. But what should he see instead? The soldier—perfectly healthy, stretched out on the silken blanket, covered with his army coat, and snoring loudly.

The servant dropped his broom and ran to his master.

"The soldier's still here and alive!" he yelled. "The devils didn't take him!"

The master couldn't believe it. So *climp-clump*, he climbed up into the tower to see for himself. Sure enough! The soldier was lying on the bed, snoring away as if nothing had ever happened.

There was only one thing unusual—the room seemed full of smoke. Puffs of it clung to the ceiling like fog. The master started coughing and the soldier yawned and opened his eyes. Then he jumped up like a shot.

"Good morning, soldier," said the master. "Have you slept well after your journey?"

"Thank you, sir. I slept very soundly."

"Didn't you dream about anything?" the master asked.

"Yes indeed! In my dream a whole dozen devils came here straight from hell. They seemed surprised to find *me* in your bedroom."

"What did you do then?"

"Oh," the soldier said calmly, "we talked all night about this and that. And I treated them to a smoke from my pipe. But something strange happened. Either the tobacco was too strong, or the devils' throats were too weak, for they smoked and smoked the pipe and never did finish it."

"Yes, yes. One can see strange things in a dream," the master remarked.

The soldier stretched and began to button his coat.

The master put on a friendly expression and said, "You don't have to rush away! Why not stay and rest another day or two in my house?"

The soldier thought, "He wants me to stay so the devils can get me. Well, I'll show him!"

But out loud he said in an agreeable voice: "Why not—as long as I have the chance? It's not often that a soldier finds a soft mattress under him."

"You are talking sense," answered the master, and he left.

The soldier again went to sleep. He slept the whole day. In the evening he got up and laid the rest of the snack on the table.

He put the bottle of wine right in the middle.

At the stroke of midnight the devils appeared. They were as angry as could be and ready to tear someone to pieces. But the soldier just smiled into his mustache. He greeted the devils as though they were old friends.

"How do you do, my dear guests! I know what you've come for!"

"Good! Then no more dilly-dallying," snapped the elder devil. "Take him, fellows."

The soldier remained calm. "I don't want to stop you from having a meal. But my grandfather always used to say, 'Dry bread will scratch your throat.' So before eating he took a sip of good wine. After that you could serve him a whole ox and he'd eat all of it! I happen to have here a small bottle of wine, and I am willing to let you have it. Drink to the bottom!"

Well, the devils did not refuse the wine. They moved in a circle up to the table and passed the bottle from one to another. It went around once and none of the wine was gone. It went around a second time—the bottle was still full. The devils drank and drank until, *limpety-lumpety*, they fell under the table one by one. But not the twelfth, the chief. He remained sitting up and kept on tippling the wine from the bottle.

Suddenly the rooster crowed outside the window.

"Hey, soldier!" shouted the older devil cheerfully. "You are in luck!" He started pushing and shaking and waking the other devils. *Swish-swush* went their tails as they all scrambled out of sight.

The master meanwhile had been turning and tossing all night. As soon as the sun was up he ran puffing

to the tower. Since the devils had left the door open, he peered into the room from the hallway. And what did he see? The soldier, sleeping soundly!

"Look at him," whispered the master. "Why won't the devils take him? I cannot understand it. But I am sure that he won't escape a third time." And he left, without waking the soldier.

On the third night, the devils were even angrier than before. Their claws were out full length when they scurried through the door. And their teeth were clicking.

"Tonight we will not let you fool us!" they screamed. "We'll tear you into little pieces before we carry you off."

"All right," said the soldier. "What's destined to happen will happen. Only let me stand in the middle of the room. If you are going to do away with me, do it at once!"

The devils moved aside, and the soldier, holding his sack, stood in the middle. Giving the sack a shake, he shouted:

"All you devils into the sack, except the chief!"

At once a hurricane seemed to sweep the room. Eleven devils spun around like tops and disappeared into the sack. Once inside, none of them made a move or a sound. Only the devil chief remained standing before the soldier.

Now it was the soldier's turn to tell the devils what to do, to demand something from *them*. What could he ask for?

The soldier shook the sack again and said to the chief: "See, all your fellow devils are trapped inside. And there's room for you, too, unless—unless you bring me three bags of gold! After you do, I'll let the little devils out and you can all go your way."

The chief devil scratched his head. "Three bags of gold doesn't seem too high a price. There's only one trouble. We have no gold. None. The master of this house has it all."

"How did that happen?" the soldier asked.

"Simple," the devil said. "The master made a contract with our leader. We gave him the gold which he was to keep for seven years. Then he was to come to this room to pay with his hide. After that, we'd get the gold back. We kept our end of the bargain, but the rich man cheated!"

"He shouldn't get away with that!" the soldier declared.

At that very moment, the door squeaked slightly, then opened and quickly slammed shut. But the soldier and the devil had enough time to recognize who was awake at such a late hour. It was the master, come to see what the devils were doing with the soldier.

"Put *him* in the sack," the devil chief suggested.

"It will serve him right," the soldier agreed. So he slapped his hand over the sack and called aloud: "Master, get in here!"

The door opened wide by itself, and the master shrieked in alarm. Then he tumbled in a somersault, spun around and around, and disappeared. The sack stretched out to make room for him.

"It's done!" said the soldier. "Now you can bring the gold here without delay."

Long before the cock budged on his roost, there were three bags in front of the soldier—all of them filled to the top with gold.

"I've swept the master's cellar clean," said the big devil. "There wasn't a coin left. Now let my friends go free."

The soldier opened the sack.

Whoosh! Out dashed the eleven little devils, dragging the rich man—heavy as he was—with them. He kicked and screamed but the devils had him in their clutches. And thus they all vanished.

As for the soldier, he had nothing to complain about. There was the big house, left by the rich

man, and the bags of gold. But the soldier didn't want to live in the gloomy old house, and three bags of gold were too heavy to carry. He decided to take only enough to fill his pockets.

But the gifts from the three old men—that was another matter. "They were all good men," the soldier thought. "And their gifts were no ordinary ones."

So when the soldier set out on the road once more, he took with him the pipe and the bottle and the sack. He might meet a stranger who would make good use of them. Or perhaps he would have need of them himself. For who could tell? Someday a dozen devils might cross his path again.

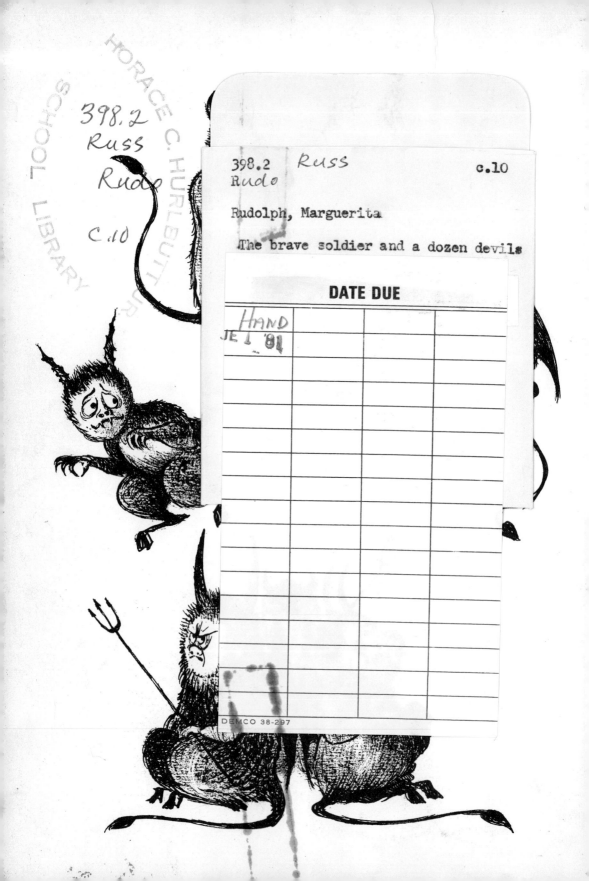

DATE DUE

HAND			
JE 1 '81			

DEMCO 38-297